I0876016

BIBLIO

SHORTS

SEVEN STORIES ABOUT TAMMY

SEVEN STORIES ABOUT TAMMY

ELIZABETH McCRACKEN

BIBLIOASIS
Windsor, Ontario

1

"**HER NAME IS TAMMY**," Morris had announced ahead of time, which is what threw his family off. They imagined Tammy, Morris's first girlfriend, first to be brought home anyhow, as a girl in a bikini who he'd met in Tallahassee, a model, he told his family, who filled in the rest. Hair in pigtails, a vacationing Iowan, a girl who'd blow over, a girl you could be teased about for the rest of your life. When Morris came home from Florida it was not with a girl but a woman. This Tammy—the actual Tammy—had thick blond hair she wore in a mid-neck bob whose depth could be measured with a ruler. Hair like the sphinx.

Tan like the sphinx. A smoker's voice: ruined? No, sexy and persuasive. Morris was twenty-seven. She wasn't.

Immediately the parlor game was *how old is she?* and Dennis, the father of them all, decided he would win.

"It's a pleasure to meet you," Tammy said.

He took her hand and palpated it. "I'm Dennis," said Dennis. This was years ago, in the old house, with the oak dining room table on the rickety sunporch, the rumbling pocket doors and skewed everything that gave the downstairs the feel of an ocean filled with ships, future wrecks, the white sofa with the mashed cushions, the china-filled dresser missing half its pulls. Soon they would live in a new house, though Dennis had not told them that yet: he'd come into some money. He was a family man and his thoughts should have been plural, *they* had come into money, Dennis and Miriam and the children. But it had been his father's money and therefore he said to himself *mine*. Victoria was a senior in high school and Porter in eighth grade. Morris and Tammy were just passing through, staying in a hotel in the Back Bay, certainly paid for by Tammy, who had an air of wealth: small gold earrings, long navy wool coat. That hair, which must have cost money to maintain. Dennis didn't know these things, being secretly rich himself. The rich never know the cost of anything. His wife, Miriam, knew.

They had never met anyone from Florida, only people who ended up there, as if by gravity. Tammy was tall and angular, stood with her hands in her own back pockets—blue jeans, ironed. Morris's jeans were ironed now, too. By her? Or had she put Morris to work at the ironing board? She seemed like that sort of woman, efficient and ruthless, with beautiful manners. There was a moment in that first ten minutes that she might have put them, Morris's family—parents, brother, sister, the family beagle Albert—to work. Set them right. Everything would have been different if they'd been obedient. Tammy might have saved them all, not just Morris. Morris wouldn't have drifted away. Porter, his brother, wouldn't've drunk so. (Of course he would've, but maybe to more charming effect.) Their parents wouldn't've argued. Victoria's life would have been changed most of all. She was seventeen then, a fool for charismatic women.

They looked at Tammy, their first stranger. They offered her the middle of the sofa. Not even Morris sat down next to her. It was 7 p.m., start of November, mid 1970s. Nobody yet understood their own properties in this particular group of people.

"Well," said Tammy, on that white sofa. "What would you like to know?"

She gestured at her own lap, and the family realized that she meant, incredibly, about herself, and they decided they already knew everything there was.

"I'm on duty," said Dennis, and he went to the kitchen to cook and drink.

The name *Tammy* didn't suit her, but it wasn't like *Albert.* Albert was a girl dog, not a boy, and had been named in a fit of exasperation after the tall serious neighbour down the street, an Episcopalian minister with the first goatee any of them had ever seen who was so full of God's love the family couldn't keep themselves from making fun. *Albert* was chosen in the usual way, every family member offering a name, alternately earnest, pretentious, absurd: *Héloise, Fathead, Cora, Darling, Ladybird, Grandma, Lucrezia Borgia, Peanut Butter,*

Chicken Kiev, Gidget, Missy, Mommy, Albert. Albert was offered and seized in a panic when it seemed the dog might really, truly, be called Mommy. Throw Albert the human to the dogs! thought the mother, whose name was Miriam. Albert did always seem a godly dog after that. By *godly* they meant serious of expression and soulful of howl and given to eating her own shit.

Miriam looked at Tammy: soft at the jaw, unwrinkled but the threat all round her face, green veins visible at the backs of her hands. The air of money led Miriam to assume she was well-preserved, as opposed to careless in her youth. An ironing board of a woman, Tammy, articulated in some places but not others, stiff, useful for one or two particular things. Adjustable but inflexible. She and Morris both wore white shirts with their dark jeans, as though they were a musical duo, or specialized missionaries, her collar turned up, his spread out.

"Dinnertime!" called Dennis.

The children of the family went to the kitchen. It was a dance both choreographed and improvised, the elbow to the swinging door, the laying down of mats on the table. Tammy held back. "No," said Miriam, in response to what? "You're our guest. Sit, sit."

"Where do you want me?"

"Anywhere," said Miriam, trying to mean it.

Tammy—handsome, elegant—looked over the table, chose a chair, failed the test. She sat in their mother's place, next to their father. When Morris delivered his last load from the kitchen, Tammy directed him to the chair across from her. Easier to communicate silently across the table, thought Miriam, who herself had been a spy at other people's dinner tables. When you sit next to your confederate everyone can read your code.

"Where in Florida?" Dennis said, as he sat down.

"You wouldn't know it," said Tammy.

"I know everything," he told her.

"Ah *ha*," said Tammy, with admiration. But he'd wanted to demonstrate the everything he knew.

Albert the dog sat on Tammy's feet under the table. "Hello, you," she said to the dog.

"Albert," said Morris. "Manners."

"She's all right," said Tammy.

"She just wants to be loved," said Miriam, embarrassing everyone. Love wasn't a topic for the dinner table in their house.

Tammy said, "Oh, Albert. *I* love you." She straightened her silverware, and looked unhappy.

Morris lifted the tablecloth, then grabbed the dog by her collar and pulled her out. "Get along, Albert," he said. Roughly, tenderly, he gathered her in his arms and carried her to the back door and let her through.

When he returned, Tammy said, gently, "Mo."

"Hmm?"

"Hands," she said, and rubbed hers together.

"Ah yes." He went to the kitchen to wash them.

Dennis had cooked dinner, seafood in béarnaise sauce in puff pastry, scallops in bacon, asparagus in bacon and butter, so much butter the air shone with it. His sauces were always breaking, and he left the kitchen streaked with roux and red wine, but he loved to cook so they agreed he had a gift for it. Miriam's own cooking ran to stuffed peppers and chili. One look at Tammy and you knew she was a health nut.

"This looks wonderful," said Tammy miserably, her fork looking for a way in.

"I'm a real butter and egg man," Dennis said.

"That's what you always say," said Porter, age thirteen. "I still don't know what it means."

"It's a quote."

"Explaining nothing," said Porter. He eyed the glasses of wine around the table. Sometimes he was allowed at dinner parties to have a drink. His father disapproved, but his mother insisted that this was why nobody in her family was a drunk. They'd learned how to handle liquor at an early age. Porter had grown six inches in the past year. He was voracious; he might never get enough of anything. The family knew it, that the once ordinary, delightful child intended to devour them all, not because he wanted to eat *them*, just the whole world that they happened to be in. The question was how to slow him down.

Tammy said, to Dennis, "You're a real French chef."

"I dabble."

"Well, if this is *dabbling*," she said. She thought she was an invited guest. She was a contestant.

Sometimes drink made an odd encyclopedia of feeling rise up inside of Dennis, voluminous and leatherbound. He was childish, more childish the older his children got. He didn't want to be outshone or outfucked. He thought he'd like to sleep with her—he hadn't known, before this moment, that he would always want to seduce his children's . . . what would you call them. He'd just never had the chance before.

Not sleep with. Snog, maybe, as the English would say. Enrapture. Win over.

The uses of her bob were clear, the way her hair fell and obscured her face, then swung back into place. With long hair it would have been intolerable, but she wielded her bob like a lady with a fan in the olden days, folding and unfolding it.

"Was he always such a talented actor?" Tammy asked.

Dennis pointed encouragingly at her plate. "Who."

"Your son. *Morris*."

"He dabbled," said Miriam.

"He's very good," said Tammy. "He's better than you know."

"I know *everything*," said Dennis again.

"I didn't know you were acting, Morris," said Miriam. "I thought you were working as a waiter."

"At a dinner theatre," said Tammy. "I'm the manager. He'll be in *The Man Who Came to Dinner* next month."

"Who keeps kicking me?" said Dennis, and in looking under the table knocked over a full glass of red wine into Tammy.

She sat for a moment. Her white shirt, which had looked like a sail on a yacht, now was the flag pirates raised to warn other boats. What would she do, take it in good humour or weep or wait to be rescued—though nobody, including Morris, was coming to her rescue, not even Albert, who scratched at the back door like a family curse.

Tammy said, in a flat voice, "Oops-a-daisy."

"Victoria," said Miriam, "take her upstairs. Get her some clothing—you can go into my closet."

Tammy gave Miriam a look which conveyed her exact measurements and her personal taste—Miriam was short and, in those days, bosomy. She had dressed for their guest in a caftan. *I will not partake in a caftan*,

Tammy's eyebrows said, and she looked over the table, measuring everyone—her eyes lingered on plump Victoria—and then said, "Porter."

"Yes?"

"You'll have something I can borrow."

"Like—like my suit?"

"Jeans," she said. "A t-shirt."

"I have those." He looked at his mother. "But what about—"

"I won't need underwear," said Tammy.

Morris went up with them, to supervise, and when they came back down—Tammy in a pair of red corduroys worn fretless at the knee, and a plaid flannel shirt tucked in, and a belt, she looked ludicrous, resplendent—he explained they would be going back to the hotel. *Oh, were you here, Morris,* his family thought.

"She's got to be in her forties," said Miriam once they'd left.

"No," said Dennis. "No."

"At least."

"I was sitting close up," said Dennis. "Thirties, though."

"Forties," said Miriam. "I will bet money."

"How do we find out?"

"She's not," said Porter. "It's sun damage."

"What?"

"That's what she told me. Because of Florida."

"How did that come up?"

"I don't know. She told me that. Why she might look a little old."

"Well *that's* suspicious," said Dennis.

"She said it to the mirror, not me."

"I didn't like her," said Victoria.

"Me neither," said Porter.

"No?" said Dennis.

"She was flirting with you, Daddy. All through dinner."

"Really?" he said. "She must have been trying to make a good impression."

"She didn't," said Victoria.

"She did not," said Miriam.

"Well, we'll never see her again," said Dennis.

"Wrong," said Miriam, and then in voice of prophecy, "That's our first child gone."

2

THEY WERE MARRIED at a VFW hall: no dancing, not enough food, a cash bar, a handful of guests. The groom had made the arrangements. Tammy, thank god, had not worn white, but a light brown suit with lapels that looked like clubs, the kind on playing cards. Morris wore a nice blue suit, with a thick blue knit tie that looked like an expensive sock. His best man was a little chinless guy who was from Texas and liked to talk about it. No maid of honor, no flower girl, no ring bearer. The Texan was it. Miriam disapproved. She would have disapproved if there had been a cast of dozens. She disapproved of the wedding, and that disapproval suffused all its particulars: the paltry guest list, the menu of spinach pie and grape leaves from the Armenian grocery store. She and Dennis had paid the bill but were not otherwise consulted. Half an hour before the ceremony started Tammy revealed that they'd been legally married the week before at City Hall. This was just theatre and revelry. The tables were square, Miriam observed sadly. They should have been round.

"I like Texans," her husband told the Texan. "Texans understand irony. You do understand that it's just a state, right? Like Delaware is a state."

Dennis had taken off his suit jacket, rolled up his sleeves. The VFW hall had gone to his head. The Texan had a thin mustache and bad teeth. He was a professor of Texan literature.

"That's a thing?" said Dennis.

"We aren't rubes and cowboys, no matter easterners think we're parochial hayseeds."

"Well, thinking your state has a literature all its own—" said Dennis, and Miriam, without planning to, said, "How old is she?"

"Who," said the Texan. "Tammy?"

"She dudn't mean Katherine Anne Porter," said Dennis.

At that the Texan smiled unhandsomely. "Couldn't say."

"Couldn't *rightly* say," said Dennis, in a bad accent. The Texan shook his head and rattled the ice in his drink. The bride and groom had sat in the middle of the hall at their own little table, and now went table to table like royalty visiting every island in a distant archipelago. They were sober. They were always sober. Dennis and the Texan were drunk or drunkish, and each thought the other a fool who could be put right through politeness.

"So you know Tammy from where," said Dennis.

"Texas," explained the Texan. "Corpus. *Christie*."

"She's a Texan?"

"Sixth generation."

"I thought Florida."

"Tammy? No. Lived there a long time, though."

"We thought Florida." Dennis turned to Miriam. "Didn't we?"

"A native Floridian," said Miriam, for the pleasure of saying the word.

"No, ma'am," said the Texan.

"How long? Did she live in Florida."

"Who knows," said the Texan.

"You know in Massachusetts we don't count generations," said Dennis. "We don't even *have* an adjective."

"That's because y'all's state is so small people keep getting shoved out the back door into Upstate New

York. Tammy and Moe'll end up in Texas, I bet. I'm a seventh generation Texan myself."

Morris and Tammy still lived in Florida. Florida—Miriam had been drinking, Miriam was not herself—Florida basically *was* Texas, wasn't it. One of those states with a panhandle and too much sunshine.

The Texan said, "Texans like to get back to Texas, in my experience."

"Back to the family ranch," said Dennis.

"Dime store," said the Texan. "Family dime store."

At that Dennis stood up. "There should be dancing. Isn't this a wedding? Aren't we paying for it? I got quarters and there's a jukebox right over yonder. There shall be dancing, goddammit."

"You're paying for it?" said the Texan to Miriam once Dennis had left.

"Well, it's not much. Though I always thought her family was rich."

"Tammy's? No, ma'am. That store's been near failing since the turn of the century."

"She *seems* rich," said Miriam. "She's got an aura of money."

"Money does not have an aura," said the Texan. "It's money. It's a fact."

"Morris would never live in Texas," said Miriam.

"Well, ma'am, you might be surprised."

"Ma'am," she said. "You think that's charming."

"I think it's polite. Other people find it charming. Tammy!" he said. "Moe! We were just speaking of you." Here they came, the happy couple. The Texan stood up and threw his napkin on the table with a flourish, as though he'd defeated it. "Congratulations."

Where was her husband? Trying to convince the bartender to plug in the jukebox. When they were out in public and he was behaving badly it was her job, she felt, to steer. *Do not go into the ditch, do not go into the ditch.* Her job to interrupt; to pat his arm to remind him that he was a family man, think of us if not yourself, it's not too late. Now Miriam got up and hugged Morris, plush and handsome Morris, who didn't belong in Texas. She wouldn't let him go.

"Mother," said Morris, who'd never called her such a thing. "Thank you for everything."

"Is—have you done something to your voice?" she asked.

"What do you mean?"

"It's deeper. Different. It makes you *look*—"

"I've been working with a voice coach," he said. "On my accent."

"You don't have an accent," she said. Then she remembered it, that tiny flag of Massachusetts that had raised itself in his vowels, now gone.

"Porter's drunk," he told her. He pointed with his chin: his younger brother sat up at the bar in his own suit, which he'd outgrown since its purchase a month before. He held himself like a stack of books. At any moment all his components might start sliding and he'd end up a pile on the floor.

"Oh," she said. Then, "Maybe he's not." He was sixteen. He shouldn't be drunk. She was his mother and responsible, though she rummaged in her brain to find a way to blame Tammy.

Tammy kissed her on both cheeks, that kind of physical affection that Miriam particularly disliked: pure obligation. They held each other's elbows.

"I love your son," Tammy told Miriam.

Miriam thought, *Jesus*. But she was the nice parent. "Thank you," she told Tammy. "Thank you for doing that."

Then Dennis's jukebox threat came true, and the music kicked in, and for some reason he had chosen *In the Ghetto*. Miriam could feel Tammy's unhappiness in her elbow grip, and then Tammy leaned in and said into Miriam's ear, "Of course we hope to have children."

"What?"

Tammy's breath was as soft and insubstantial as health food. "We hope to give you grandchildren."

Miriam wanted to say, Oh? Where will you get them? Tammy was not bad for fifty, or however old she was, but her new husband was just thirty and Miriam wanted them to plan for a life of realism. She didn't like being drafted into games of pretend.

"Well," she said into Tammy's ear. It was easier not seeing her face, easier to say things under the cloak of Elvis. "We'll see."

"We're praying for them."

"You're *praying*," said Miriam. She leaned back and looked at Tammy's face, the little swaths of wrinkles on either side of her mouth, the whole palpable middle age of her. All this while—three years—Miriam had thought, *I can't ask her. How can I ask her?* "How old are you?" she said now.

"Morris and I are of an age."

You couldn't call somebody a liar. Miriam couldn't. If Dennis were here, he might, or he would laugh and shake his head. Across the hall Dennis was trying to dance with an old lady to *In the Ghetto*, a waltz to a ballad, a victory dance, though the song was already ending. Miriam could only wait for Tammy to release her elbows, to return her to the inane Texan.

"We'll go pretty soon," said Tammy. "You all stay. We have the hall till eleven."

You all. It was a con, thought Miriam. For three years, Tammy had been coming to visit them and every time she had sat with Albert the beagle, never helping in the kitchen, never picking up a plate, talking only about Morris. Her first born! Her favourite child, though of course that was a secret, how could he not be, she had spent so long looking uninterrupted into his face, his eyes as they'd passed from pale blue to hazel brown, as his skinny legs—he'd been born scrawny, six pounds—had acquired rolls and his arms cuffs of fat. Of her younger children she remembered mostly them saying, *look, mommy, look,* and she had then, she had looked, but it was always away from Morris.

Look, here came Porter, led by his sister, plump Victoria with the beautiful legs she knew how to show off, *look*. Porter *was* drunk. Even his hair was drunk. What nobody had told Miriam about motherhood, that the bodies of her children would feel like her own body. Not in any poetic way, not that she felt their pain or their ecstasy. Only shame and pride, vanity and self-loathing.

"In the ghetto!" said Porter. He looked like he wanted to add something, but the words were coins on the floor and he knew if he bent to pick them up, he'd go over.

"You're leaving?" Miriam said to Tammy.

"Yes. Any moment." She touched Morris's hand—Morris! her husband! Morris, a husband!—and he put his arm around her waist.

"We going?" he said to her. "Well, Ma—"

Was he going to run down the list of possibilities? Was this an acting thing, an accent thing, *Maman, Mutter, Mam, Madre, Mere*—

Across the floor Dennis was talking to the old lady. He looked sweet, pacific, though his hand rattled in his pocket for more quarters. Miriam felt his cast-off bad behavior settle around her shoulders. This happened sometimes. When he was away from her she found herself heading straight for the ditch, full of joy and destruction. Morris was wonderful, blockheaded: if Tammy said she was young enough to have children, he would believe her.

She said, "Take Porter home on your way."

Tammy said, "I don't think—"

"It's not like it's your *real* wedding night," said Miriam.

Morris looked at Tammy first, then his mother. He'd always been so easily confused. "Yes it is," he said.

"I won't pry your father away for an hour. Porter needs to go home. You're going that way anyhow. Everyone's already been deflowered, is my guess."

"Christ," said Tammy.

"OK," said Morris.

"Thank you," said Miriam. She sat down. Everyone was looking at her. She couldn't sort out what they were thinking and she didn't care. "Are you a well-known scholar?" she asked the Texan. "The foremost?"

"I am famous in Texas which is good enough for Texans, which is good enough for me," said the Texan, and then, "I guess he's marrying his mother."

"I guess he is," said Morris's mother, and her unmarried children were terrified to see the joy shining on her face.

3

VICTORIA DECIDED SHE would distinguish herself by being the one Harkin known for her kindness, her openness. She tried to relate to Tammy that way.

"Look at you, girl!" said Tammy, ruining it. "So skinny! You're beautiful."

"I wax and wane like the moon," said Victoria.

Which was true all her life, she gained weight and lost it, plump, fat, slender—never actually skinny, no matter what Tammy said. People treated you differently, depending on your size, but Victoria always felt entirely herself, the same, she just emitted different noises, like the bars of a xylophone when struck.

They were in Philadelphia, 1991. Tammy and Morris had lived in Center City for a year. Victoria had moved to the city the month before—she was getting a master's degree in psychology at Drexel—and she lived in large apartment on the third floor of a semidetached house at 48th and Springfield. This morning she'd come home from her run to see her first-floor neighbour sitting on the front steps, as he often was. He was a man in his fifties, blond the way babies are. "Halt," he'd said, "there's been a break-in."

From the knob up the front door was intact and itself, but the bottom half had been entirely shattered. It didn't look like the work of human strength; it would have to be a wild animal of the folktale variety, or the sort of sudden storm that rearranges livestock in the Midwest, picks up a set of pigs in the countryside and lets them off, like hitchhikers, where it wants to, not where's convenient for the pigs. "He must have really wanted whatever was inside," said the neighbour, Joe, and Victoria had reflexively wanted to say, "Or her," as was her habit. "Must have," she said instead. He must have wanted it, though all he took was a hundred dollar bill that Joe had suspended on his refrigerator with a magnet, like a mouse removing a rhombus of cheese from a trap. Victoria's apartment had been untouched.

She did not call her parents to report this story. She didn't tell anyone. As long as she said nothing, the upper half of her was intact, still locked, like the door.

Morris and Tammy lived in a high rise across the river from the train station and had invited her for dinner and Tammy had answered the door and exclaimed over Victoria and brought her into the living room, which had floor to ceiling windows that looked west, over the universities of University City, and further west. That's why a high rise. Victoria understood and despised her understanding.

"Isn't it nice," said Tammy.

"It's quite a view," said Victoria, who'd been trained by her mother.

The living room was one sofa and a variety of cushions on the floor, pulled up to the coffee table, which seemed to be a chunk of farm machinery topped by a giant piece of glass. These days Tammy was an interior decorator. Morris was acting, mostly sea captains and villains at a local children's theatre, though he took the train to New York for auditions, hoping for something better, and came home and cooked and did the housework. Now he brought out shallow bowls of soup. He wore a manly apron that looked to be meant for smithery of some kind, but the soup was delicate, delicious: a smooth substance made of mushrooms and vegetable stock and a hint of peanut. "It's so good!" said Victoria. She'd lost the weight mostly through hours of swimming at the Drexel pool and the speed she bought from Brian, the neighbour. The speed wasn't an everyday thing, just weekends, a new habit. She snorted it. Her nose was sore. Even now it was.

"Do you want more?" asked Tammy in a friendly way.

"Oh, no thank you!" she said. "I'm saving room for dinner."

In the pause that followed she understood that this *was* dinner. There was no further course, not so much as a cheese plate. She began in her head to tell the story to her mother. Mortification could be useful, if you could convert it to a story, this was the lesson of her childhood, though usually you had to sit with the mortification a while to be able to soften it up enough to fashion it into something for somebody else to admire.

"I'm having more!" said Morris jovially. "You, too, Vic?"

My handsome brother, she thought. The family spoke of Tammy as though she'd kidnapped Morris from a playground in order to raise him as her own child, but he'd been a grown-up, and clearly life with Tammy suited him. He had not been good-looking as a kid but he was a handsome man, with thick hair cut expensively by somebody—a dour old man barber, or a dour young woman stylist, Victoria guessed—who also attended to his eyebrows and beard. Even his nose looked different. Before Tammy, it had tended to the piggy—nostril-prominent, bunched bridge—and the change wasn't surgical but in the way he held his head and how he no longer viewed the world with alarm.

"More soup, Vic?"

Victoria wasn't sure what the right answer was. She picked up her bowl and tried to stand up from her cushion. Across the coffee table, Tammy accomplished this as though on hydraulics, saying *sit, sit*, as she went up. "And then we have something we want to show you. Why we asked you here."

She *had* wondered. What could they want from her? She was seized with fear: an egg. They wanted to have a baby but Tammy was too old and they wanted an egg that would be family. The idea disgusted her. Also it didn't make sense: you couldn't do that with a brother and sister. It had to be something else. They had given her a glass of white wine that tasted green as a tree, with an aftertaste of violin. Who knows how long it had been in the fridge.

“All right!” said Tammy. “Here’s what we want to show you.”

She had a videotape in her hand, and she slid it into the player.

“This is important,” she said. “Self defence. Have you ever heard of model mugging?”

Victoria shook her head. “You were a model, weren’t you?”

Tammy laughed and touched her throat. She was never so happy as when other people were stupid. “No,” she said. “I mean, I was, but not that kind of model. You need to learn how to defend yourself. I want you to watch this.”

On the television, a class of women stood next to a man who was wearing an enormous padded suit the dimensions of a cartoon character at a theme park. He held a large blank head under his arm, then attached it to the padded suit. His actual head—its mustache and shaggy hair—disappeared, and he was no longer human. He was robot, or a zombie swollen from an allergic reaction. A series of little plays ensued. A member of the class would pretend to walk down the street, and the padded monster would follow and then touch the woman on the shoulder. One by one the women attacked, screaming, NO! and STOP! NO! They kneed him in his padded stomach, kicked him in his padded groin. Victoria had always imagined self-defence classes as silent and elegant; *imagined* meaning seen on television. The women in the model mugging course took pleasure in attacking their enormous would-be rapist. NO! DON'T! In her head Victoria saw the shattered door of her building. Whoever had done that might do anything he liked. To be pummelled to death: at least she would feel the hands of strangers upon her, all she ever wanted. In Philadelphia she drank too much and snorted speed on the weekends and filled her closets with recycling, bottles of beer in one and stacks of newspapers in another, she never remembered what day or where to take them and it had been months. It was as though Philadelphia were a forest she'd been abandoned in the middle of; she'd never felt so alone in all her life. Years later she would realize that the feeling was adulthood. Nobody had told her she'd reached it.

Victoria saw that Tammy was among the students, hard to recognize because she wore a gray tracksuit and a blue baseball cap and looked like an old woman. It was her turn. She attacked the man in the suit, who was like a toddler, big-headed and big-bottomed, with limbs the brain couldn't properly operate. GET AWAY! Tammy on the TV bellowed. "I'm the best student," Tammy on the cushion told Victoria, and Victoria could see that this wasn't so. Her aim was true. Her fists were weak. "I can take you to a class."

"Maybe."

When it was over, Tammy said, "I have clothing. I was going to donate it to charity but it'll fit you now, it'll be good for job interviews, some lovely stuff."

The bedroom had the same view: river, train station, west and more west. The curtains were open. Why not? Nobody could see in. Victoria imagined the streets filled with model muggers stalking ordinary women: the silence of the hulking blank attackers, the shouts of the attacked. In her head the attackers were even bigger, nosing through Philadelphia like mice in a maze.

"Here," said Tammy, handing her a pair of black jeans and a suede blazer and a peachy silk blouse.

"All right," Victoria said, and headed for the bathroom.

"Where are you going," said Tammy, "we're both girls, you can change here."

Neither were girls. Victoria was twenty-four and Tammy was—how old *is* she, Victoria's mother kept asking, fixated. Tammy had a deep line between her eyebrows and her earlobes seemed ripe, like stone fruit. Victoria could not bear the idea of revealing herself, her various stretchmarks, the unshaved and untended neighbourhoods of her body, all the evidence of neglect and intemperance, but she couldn't see a way out of it. She turned her back to Tammy but there was no shielding herself: the closet doors were mirrored. Tammy's panopticon.

"I was fucked up when I was young," Tammy said.

"What?"

"Probably I'm still fucked up."

In the mirror Tammy looked frightened for Victoria, as though this night would decide everything.

But straight on she looked like herself, acid and inexorable. “You look so beautiful,” Tammy said, and Victoria could see in the closet’s sliding mirror door that it wasn’t true. Her face had broken out in weird blossoms, from the swimming pool or from the speed. Epidermal confusion; her own human hide. Her hair was uncombed. She was smaller than she had been, that was true. It seemed a mistake God had made, that you could change sizes like this.

The story Victoria would tell to her mother about this night was snagged and laddered, a mess.

“Not quite,” said Tammy, frowning at Victoria’s hips. All of West Philadelphia looking through the window, frowning.

None of the clothing fit. It was all too long, too tight. Tammy might as well have brought a tape measure to the dinner table. Dear me, dear me: not quite, no good.

4

IT SEEMED TO PORTER that he was always drunk and in the back seat of a car, Morris driving, Tammy showing her pinch-pot profile. Tammy despised Porter. He knew that from his first backseat ride, away from their wedding. He's older now, Porter, older than Morris then and older than his father lived to be, and now he has to acknowledge that it was odd, his mother insisting that the bride and groom drive the groom's little brother home from the wedding. They should have driven off to their own life together, waving from a carriage. But instead they put him in the back of their Toyota. That night, he had the hiccups like a little drunk from a cartoon, with a red nose, tipping a crushed hat at parking meters.

"I can't believe your mother," said Tammy.

"It's not a big deal."

"It's a big deal to me. I wasn't ready to leave."

"Honey! You said you were ready."

Porter had the sort of hiccups that actually made him say Hic. "Hic," he said from the backseat.

"Jesus," said Tammy.

They pulled up to the family house—the new one, which everyone hated. The bride and groom were arguing but in voices of love. Porter tried to open the door but he couldn't. He was the level of drunk that made him wish he had a mirror to look at himself in order to marvel at how drunk he was. Assess, too, but mostly marvel.

"It was a battle between us," said Tammy. She touched the side of Morris's face. He'd shaved off his beard for the wedding, a mistake. "And you let her win. On this day, this one day, you should have made clear you were on my side."

"I *am* on your side. Who else's?"

"I worried about this ahead of time." She shook her head.

"Oh, sweetheart," said Morris. "I am—you're right."

"I know it."

"What can I do now?"

She shrugged. Her shoulders were bare: she had taken off the jacket and set it like a sleeping baby in the trunk of the car.

"We're here now."

"We're here now," she agreed.

Porter couldn't open the car door. At first he thought it was the drink—one of the things he liked about drinking, the funhousification of the stupid world, how it bent corridors and spun beds. He loved the sense of upheaval. But he wasn't *that* drunk. He tried the handle again.

"Your mother loves you, I guess," Tammy said. "But she plays favourites."

"Does she?" asked Morris.

"She's never been to one of your plays."

"In high school—"

"I mean lately," she said.

"She was going to. Before *Hornby* closed."

"That wasn't your fault," she said. "You were wonderful."

"Thank you, sweetheart."

"When you're famous she'll regret it."

"Maybe."

"I mean, you're *known*. You're known *now*."

Something had shifted, Porter realized. They were putting on a conversation for his benefit, and yet he had also disappeared.

He tried the door again, but as though he were at a play himself he felt he must be silent till it ended. He pulled the handle, gentled it back into place, pulled, gentled.

"*Hornby* should have been a big deal," said Tammy.

"It could be revived." Morris yawned, his knuckles against his mouth, and Porter gave an answering yawn that he couldn't keep quiet.

"Well, I'm not tucking you into bed," said Tammy.

"You're not," said Morris, hurt.

"Not you!" she said, "him."

They had remembered him! Thank god. "Can't open the door," Porter said, joyfully.

"You fucking *baby*," said Tammy, in a mild voice. She said it for the same reason she might get mad at an actual baby: what were the odds he'd remember?

She undid her seat belt and reached across him. Her bare arm was fragrant, almondy. Porter felt like he should do something. Lick it. Bite it. Her upper arm went past him. He felt suffused with love for her, he understood why Morris adored her, her bossy anger. Yes, he was a fucking baby. Her fingertips caught the handle. Nothing. He kissed her shoulder and she withdrew her arm as though spring loaded like the seatbelt, both all at once and inch by inch.

Was it that kiss—a joke to himself, what's the dumbest mistake you can make at this moment with the materials you have to hand—was it that which sealed his fate, which convinced Tammy to convince Morris to convince his parents to send him to Idaho to a camp for wayward boys for the summer? Rehab, said his first girlfriend, a few years later. Oh, god no, said Porter, punishment. I was sent away. Poor kid, said the girlfriend, who didn't want to hear anything more, in case what had happened would change her feelings about it. It was the worst time in my life, he said. I can't bear it, said the girlfriend, and she was telling the truth.

Tammy's face told him the mistake he'd made.

He fiddled with the handle. This time he let it thunk. "Child lock's on," he told the roof of the car. "Somebody'll have to get out to help me."

5

THINGS HAPPENED OVER the Tammy years. Albert the beagle was middle-aged when she and Tammy met; they loved each other. Albert knew they were both likely to be put in the backyard. The Harkins would say, of either one of them, Well of *course* you're a member of the family, but it wasn't true. Neither Albert or Tammy *wanted* it to be true. The fur of Albert's belly was white when they met, a loose rug a pleasure and a catastrophe as she slid on it. But her hips grew rusty and she herself forgetful. She could not be left outside in the cold; she wore a little red coat for walks, and then boots; her eyes turned to opals and she barked at shadows. She refused all food but hot dogs. She peed on the rug. She died. She was replaced, infuriatingly, by a large ginger cat called Colonel Pickering.

Dennis was middle-aged too; a professor of psychology at Lasell College; then, once the money from his family came in, a former professor who believed he would find his destiny. Any day now. Perhaps *he* was meant to be an actor. Or a playwright. Or meant to read books about self-actualization and become—no, he hated those books, so he would write one. He had heart attack and reformed all his bad habits for six months. One of his retinas detached and he had surgery to fix it and the doctors put a bubble of gas in his eye which meant he had to keep his head parallel to the ground while the eye healed. He drank red wine through a straw and listened to talk radio so that he could disagree with it, he told his wife, though she suspected that he didn't. One spring in 2003 his children asked him about a living will, and the old man waved the notion away and said, "I mean, I don't want to be a *vegetable*. But anything short of that . . ."

What did that mean? What's short of a vegetable? "Anyhow," said Victoria, "I don't think you're supposed to use that phrase anymore."

"To avoid offending carrots, no doubt," said Tammy, who was one of those people offended by people who told her she was offensive. Offensiveness was one of life's reliable pleasures: you couldn't make someone love you, some people refused to be frightened, but everybody—if you worked with wit and a scalpel—could have their feelings hurt. "What can he mean? His whole life has been a gun held to his head."

They didn't have to worry about nuance. He grew older and thought that the only way he might change the world was by leaving it: the world would miss him. So he did: he died, of a heart attack so sudden he fell through the floor of existence and was gone without a chance of rescue. Was not replaced.

Everyone else grew old.

6

ELENA AND PORTER spent eight Christmases at home, in San Luis Obispo, first the two of them, then with their twin daughters. Elena was an only child, and Porter longed to be. Twins were a joke and a relief: they didn't have to make a decision. Elena's parents were dead. Porter's were—not estranged, that was too strong a word for it. Not part of the equation.

Unforgiven but not unforgivable. Elena had met them three times in eight years.

A grown-up way to live, thought Elena, to be, in your thirties, already at the head of the table. But also childish, as though you were pretending. Then Porter's father died, and for the first time in years he saw his brother and sister and mother at a family event, and he came back saying, "Christmas, I think. All together."

We're always together, Elena said, to herself.

She was pregnant again, two months. Their friends with kids all had parents and siblings who babysat, sometimes for a week at a time: it might not be so bad to make nice with the family. They would go to Rhode Island for the holiday, to a house Porter's mother had rented with a view of the ocean, bedrooms and bathrooms for everyone, a room under the eaves with narrow beds for the children—meaning the twins, Leah and Samantha, who were six, since Victoria's Millie was only three months old, and Morris and Tammy were childless.

"Childless, except for each other," said Porter.

"What does that mean?" said Elena, who had met Morris but not Tammy.

"You'll see," said Porter. "They're each other's little biddle baby."

On the drive from Logan, Porter worried over which room they'd get: everyone else was already at the house. "They'll put us all in the attic," he said.

"They won't."

"When I was a child," he said, "I got the littlest room. It didn't even have central heating."

"What?" she said. "No heating in *Boston?*"

"'We have divided in three our kingdom,'" said Porter. "King Lear. But bedrooms. I'm Cordelia," he explained. "Luckily there's an ocean nearby, so I can drown myself."

The girls hadn't slept on the red-eye and were now unconscious in the backseat, would be off the entire week. Elena said, "That's Ophelia. Who drowns. Not Cordelia."

Porter said, "*I* would have liked to be an actor, too."

"You're an artist," she said. He was, an illustrator and cartoonist. Elena taught dance at a fancy private high school.

"I would have liked to be an actor," he said again.

The house was brick and ivied, up a hill. From the street you couldn't see the promised ocean view, though you could hear the water. Morris met them at the door. He had a mustache, a recent acquisition but already belonging to the ages: lush, piebald. "You remember your Uncle Morris, don't you?" he said of himself to Leah and Samantha. "No?"

They'd been three when they'd met in California.

"It's the mustache," he said to Elena. "How are you?" He kissed her cheek. Porter leaned in for a hug and Morris caught him by the shoulder and stopped him, pushed him back, assumed an expression of fondness. "Hey, kid," he said. "Merry Christmas. Let me take your bag." He led them to a room on the second floor with a view on the water and an attached bathroom. "This is you, and the girls will be upstairs, right over head. Get settled in and come downstairs."

The house was on a cliff. Ocean filled the frame of the window, magnificent, sick-inducing. Elena was from Omaha. She had never thought to be frightened of the ocean, was relieved to see that the bed was parallel to the shore, and her side of the bed—an inviolable organizing principle of their marriage—was away from it.

Downstairs you couldn't get away from the ocean, though the effect was not so dire, being lower, with a visible deck. The house was old: there would have been walls down here at some point, rooms, organization. Now the first floor was one open space, a fireplace at one end, the kitchen at the other, dining room between, windows onto the water. Victoria, Porter's sister, sat in a blue floral armchair with Millie, the baby; Morris was in the kitchen, handling a bouquet of kale so large he looked like an allegorical figure illustrating *Plenty*, or *Wealth*. Their spouses were elsewhere. Their mother was wiping down the kitchen island with a dirty blue sponge. No energy changed when Elena and Porter came into the space, as though they were ghosts. As though the Harkins were immune.

Gutted, that was the word for the house.

"Did you give us the *best* room?" Porter asked.

Victoria shrugged and kissed the baby's head. "Where are the girls?" she asked.

"They'll be down," Porter said, and Victoria told the baby, "They'll be down." The attic bedroom had a pony-sized billiard table and a stack of board games and two sets of bunk beds, so they could each sleep aloft. To sleep in a new place when you were a child was to live an alternate life, as significant as a Halloween costume.

"Hi, Ma," said Porter. His mother gave him a distant smile that got no closer when he kissed her on the cheek. But then she touched his jaw. "I'm glad you're here," she said. There was a hopeless look in her eyes that seemed to belong to a younger mother.

They didn't hear Tammy come down the stairs. She was too elegant and insubstantial, and somehow she had quieted the girls, who were ordinarily given to galumphing—Samantha particularly. They flanked Tammy; she had her arms out, fingertips touching the girls' shoulders, displaying them like angels, and she dressed in a long white shirt and white jeans. Summer in December, Florida in Maine, though she and Morris lived now in Wimberly, Texas.

"Porter," she said, warmly, warningly. "And you must be Elena." She took Elena's hand. Her fingers were spigot cold.

"Tammy," said Elena. "Of course."

Morris had put down his kale, his mustache fretful. "Did you sleep, darling?" he asked her.

Tammy shrugged. Elena felt the shrug in the clasp of her hand. She felt a charge, or attention, interest. Tammy was the only person in the room who gave off anything like it. "Your children are lovely," Tammy said. In her white clothing, she looked like a benevolent cult leader—early days of the cult, before things turned mad and all about money—and Elena thought she might do anything Tammy suggested.

"Is that true?" Porter said, herding the girls away. "Are you lovely? Come on. Let's go find the beach." He turned to the room: his mother, sister, brother, their spouses, the baby. He didn't look at his wife. He said, in a voice of disbelief, "It's good to be back."

Tammy had been described to Elena—wicked; peculiar; old, who knew what actual age—but Elena had not been prepared to feel tender. All week Tammy wore white, in a variety of fabrics, wool, denim, gauze, silk, one of those older women who have decided to follow a sartorial plan as though it were a prescription. Perhaps now that she was no longer sunbathing, she wanted to look tan. She wasn't well. Her bones asserted themselves, she'd turned the corner from slim to skeletal. Her elbows were wider than her forearms; her wristbones shone like ornaments; her cheekbones, always high and forbidding, gave her the look of a patient with a wasting disease (life was a wasting disease), though around her eyes looked padded with fat. Even her brassy hair had greened like a bell. Perhaps they should have bundled her up and put her on the porch so the cold could clear her lungs. She was sick. Old. When she'd first come to the family she'd been in her early fifties, surely, and now she was in her seventies, surely, though Morris was a youthful forty-five. She spent most of the time in their room, the door closed whether she was in it or out. When she came down she doted on Leah and Samantha.

"Come talk to me," Tammy told them. She sat on a corner of the vast sectional sofa at the far end of the main room, the part with the footrest. "I can hold a conversation. Unlike a *baby*."

"You don't like babies," Leah said.

"Not much," said Tammy, patting the sofa on either side of her, *come come*.

"She's just a little *baby*," Samantha explained, but they got onto the sofa under her arms, left and right.

"Plenty of room," she said. "No, a baby isn't an interesting person. *You*, on the other hand, are interesting people." They nuzzled their heads against her.

She could be off-putting, too, of course. She said, "Leah and Samantha. What a funny combination of names." And, "Well you're certainly not *identical* twins." They weren't: different heights, and shapes, and hair color, and they could tell the way she said it that one of them was preferable, looks-wise, probably Leah, who was taller, and thinner, though Samantha had the green eyes Tammy approved of.

"Oh, the baby's in a strop again," said Tammy. "Don't listen to her, girls. *We* don't have to wait on her."

Millie, the baby, was serious when she wasn't wailing, in the period of infancy when she could go from being pink and dry to covered up to the back neck in soft yellow shit, down to the middle of her chest in milky vomit. She had a bumpy rash on her cheek and visible cradle cap, as though she were turning to wax. Samantha and Leah watched her the way they watched the fire, respectfully, fascinated, batted away by grown-ups when they leaned too close in. They snuck their hands to her cheeks when nobody was looking. They talked baby talk to her. Everyone had expected them to be jealous of the baby, but they weren't the ones.

"*Baby* talk," said Tammy, as though the word *baby* were a slur.

It was as though Tammy were a ghost, too. Victoria bounced the baby absent-mindedly on her knee; her sweet bland husband, Ben, wore the baby strapped to his chest facing out, he the parachute, she the prodigy skydiver, flapping, flapping, a daredevil. Ben could be heard and noticed. The girls, too. Even Porter could be picked up on the family radio, after some minor tuning. Elena stopped trying to be perceived. She let Porter speak for her, fill her plate at meals, complain to her at night in the bed under the crashing baffle of the ocean.

No, it wasn't that Porter's mother was unforgiving, thought Elena, just that she had the quiet dignity of somebody whose memory had started to rub away at the edges, who trod carefully to avoid the cliff. "Hello, darling," she said to Samantha, Leah, the baby. She smiled doubtfully at the head of the table for all meals.

"She's still mad at me," Porter said to his sister, as Elena chopped garlic. It was Porter and Elena's turn to cook that night, Victoria had made up a schedule. Porter was on deveining duty. *Deveining* meaning, *take the shit out*, pulling the dark matter out of the back of shrimp that were still a little frozen.

Ben said, "That's a lot of spice for the baby."

The baby was going to eat scampi?

"No, but *eventually*," said bland Ben, who could not say the word *breast* or *milk—milk* was worse, when it was human, and you were surrounded by in-laws.

"She's not mad," said Victoria to Porter.

Tammy stood a foot or two from the counter in a pale canvas smock and wool leggings. She looked ready for martyrdom, a wheel, a cross, a cell to be walled into. She said, "Why would she be mad?"

"She's not mad," Victoria repeated.

Tammy tapped her temple and said, "Early onset."

"Early onset *what*," said Porter.

"I wouldn't call it *early*," said Victoria. "She's nearly eighty." Then, "Her memory's not what it was."

Porter had lost track of the bowls: the one with the shrimp ready to be cleaned, the bowl of shells and guts, the one with gleaming finished shrimp. What was he holding? Where did it go? He emptied his hands onto the counter. "Can she still live alone?"

"She doesn't," said Victoria. "She lives with us."

"Since when?" said Porter.

"Porter," said Tammy. "It's high school all over again."

"What do you mean?"

"You haven't done the reading," she said. "You can't bluff your way through it."

Whatever he had done wrong, his mother had forgotten. Whatever she had done wrong, too. It was too late for everything.

—

Christmas Eve Elena stood on the deck and Tammy joined her. Even her down coat was white, segmented like a caterpillar. It was sunny and cold. Elena squinted and looked up at the house.

"Nice house," said Elena.

"It is," Tammy agreed. She sat down on one of the built-in benches. "Sneaking outside makes me want to smoke a cigarette."

"You smoke?"

"Oh, not for years," said Tammy. "I mean, occasionally. But I wouldn't here. Or around you." She gave Elena a knowing look. "You're expecting. Yes, I thought so." She indicated her own jaw line. "I can always tell." Then, "I think it's terrible, what Victoria and Ben did." There was pleasure in her eyes, in-law to in-law.

"What did they do?"

"They always do it. Took the best spot." She pointed to Victoria and Ben's room at the corner on the second floor, with its double exposure.

Elena had known all along they didn't have the best room, was full of love for her husband, the dummy, who had convinced himself. They all kept their doors closed. Now she looked at the house. "You have a balcony," she observed.

"No," said Tammy. Then, "Yes. But Ben and Victoria rushed in and took the best room." She pointed again. "Best view. On the corner. They said it was the only one with space for the baby."

"We have a good view," said Elena. "They're all good views."

"It's terrible," said Tammy, not so confidential now. She wrapped herself tighter in her white down coat, her white wool shawl. "I'm going in."

Tammy stayed in her room for the rest of the day, the door closed, right through dinner.

The next morning, Christmas, Tammy came down in her pajamas, though her pajamas—white silk—and her robe—white wool, with satin piping—were nicer than anyone else's clothing.

"Wine is flowing," she said, nodding at the champagne glasses.

She sat by the fire, built with great competence and noise by Morris. Porter was drawing pictures for his girls. Ben, Victoria's husband, watched. "Impressive," he said.

"Thanks."

The picture was a bear wearing a monocle.

"You should write a children's book," said Ben.

"Maybe," he said.

Say it, thought Elena. But she could see he couldn't: it cost him too much. She said, "Porter sold a couple of illustrations to the *New Yorker*."

"Great!" said Ben. "Porter, that's great."

Tammy said, "You know, Morris is very good at drawing, too."

"All my children are good at drawing," said Miriam, uniting three long-divided things. She was sitting in the dining room table between the kitchen and the living room. Her fingers played fretfully, musically, on the edge.

"Morris could have been an artist," said Tammy.

Elena wanted to stab her with a comb. Why a comb? Because they were in a women's prison together and that's how it worked.

Tammy had brought the girls vintage kimonos and remote-control animals, one dog, one cat, and no other present could compare. Samantha in her kimono said to Elena, "Look, mama, look!"

"What is it, honey?"

"I got a robot."

"Sorry," said Tammy, as though she'd bought the girls cartons of cigarettes, then to Samantha, "Do you like it, sweetie? I saw it in the store and I knew you had to have it."

"Why apologize?" Porter asked.

"I hope it's not too much. Is it too much?"

Porter had thought that the children would win them the love of the family: his mother, his siblings. He'd done it: gotten married and had a family. But the girls received the love directly. Elena saw. It flowed over and around him.

Miriam sat at the dining room table. People shrunk in old age but she had overdone it. Porter was the tallest person in his family, and perhaps that was the cause of the trouble. He'd been sent away for crimes of juvenile height. Because he had been sent away; that was the story of his life, one of the first things he'd told Elena, and he'd thought he might have a conversation with his mother about it.

It was too late. It would have been too late even if she remembered everything. They'd read his absence as carelessness. They believed he'd never done anything deliberately in his life.

"Mom," he said to her. One of the flaws of the house, long benches instead of dining room chairs, the better to cram people in. He threaded his legs in to sit down next to her. "Come to California."

"Oh," she said. "Why would I go to California? No. I've forgotten things. I don't—" She waved her hands to dismiss the things she'd forgotten, as though they were cluttering the table in front of her. "No more travel. Not capable. I'd like a glass of wine, I think." She looked hopefully at the bottle in front of her.

"Red or white?" said Ben.

"I've got it, Ben." Porter poured some of the left-out wine into one dirty glass for his mother, into another for himself. "You could live with us."

"Live where?"

"In California," he said.

She took his hands in her own and looked at them. She was seventy-nine. She smelled, as she had since his childhood, of over-ironed clothing. He'd imagined she would be lighter after his father's death, she'd be one of those terrible words applied to old women, *sprightly, spry.* "I only know one family in California," she said. "I know lots of families here."

Then Porter took a sip of wine. Nobody but Elena would have really known what that meant—they didn't know he hadn't had a drink in fifteen years, had never tasted a Malbec. Elena thought she could taste it herself, the particular darkness of stolen drink. Nostalgia, unhappiness, the belief that if he put himself in peril his mother would come out of herself, wherever she was, to untie him from the railway tracks, which she had done for years before he was sent away. After that was when she stopped.

He said to Tammy suddenly, "I was a child."

"Yes," she said. "We all were."

"When you sent me away."

"I didn't do that."

"Porter," said Miriam, "it wasn't—" and Morris interrupted her. "Porter, knock it off," he said, deploying his big brother voice.

"I saved your life," said Tammy. "Don't forget it."

"You didn't. You put me in *more* danger, and then I saved myself."

"So it worked."

"Did it?" said Porter.

"Look at you."

"It wasn't Tammy," said Miriam. "It was us."

Tammy sat down across the table—it took nothing to step over the bench to sit, she was a ghost, she manifested.

Maybe everything that happened afterward—Porter's self-destruction, the collapse of his marriage, the tragedy of Leah, the long unhappiness of Samantha, the loss of their house—perhaps it all grew out of Porter's spite. Or maybe it had been written in the stars, or in his DNA, the two things now indistinguishable, and Tammy had only delayed it a while.

She said, "It was me, Porter. And I'd do it again. I'd do it for any of you."

Morris and Tammy left soon after that. "To get a jump on traffic," Morris said jovially. His eyes twinkled; his new mustache drooped. Ten minutes after they pulled away, Elena stood and said, "I want to show you something."

Solemnly she led everyone else up the stairs, swung Morris and Tammy's door open to display a room twice as large as any other, with a bay window, a bathroom with a balcony, the tub with a view of the water.

It didn't make sense to be jealous of a room, the house was altogether so lovely. And yet. "They have two trash cans, and I didn't have *one*," Miriam said, and then, "I'm going to have a bath in this glorious tub."

"Me, too," said Elena. "You first, then me."

One by one, they did. They had a bath in Tammy's tub, put their healthy, joyous, petty bottoms where her bony one had had been, and from water they looked at water. Even the children, one by one.

7

"**SHE LOOKS PEACEFUL**," said Victoria.

"She is," said Morris.

He was holding Tammy's hand. She'd fallen down their front stairs a week before, but she'd been dying before that. She was in bed, unconscious, but whether she was asleep or blanketed by morphine or in an actual coma, Victoria didn't know and couldn't ask. Beneath her navy-blue quilt, Tammy looked like a reliquary for her own broken bones.

Morris had pulled out all the scrapbooks of Tammy's life, of their life together and Tammy's life before Morris, and Victoria missed her mother with foolish passion. The answer to the enduring question of Tammy's age could be found here, surely. Miriam had died two months before, at eighty. Victoria picked up one of the books. Young womanhood: Tammy as a dancer, before she'd adopted the bob, her blond hair to her shoulders, her body liquid, from the *Corpus Christi Caller-Times*. The date torn off. All the dates torn off and Tammy young and beautiful. Victoria looked at Tammy in the bed, and she was beautiful now, too, in the same way, all the things that had ever constricted her face, competition and pride, gone. "She's so full of herself!" Victoria once said to her mother, and Miriam had said, "No, it's a lack of self-esteem that makes her act that way. People who hate themselves make such a lot of noise to hide it."

Victoria knew that was true and it made her furious. Why should she feel sorry for the bullies and braggarts of the world, when she had her own one-layer self-loathing to attend to? Worse, what if that was her, too?

"Darling," said Morris.

"What?" said Victoria.

"Ah!" said Morris. "No. I—would you get me a glass of water?"

They were the closest of the siblings despite the age difference which meant they hadn't been young together. He'd had a whole childhood as an only child. What had their parents been doing in the nine years between them? Doting. Deliberating. Suffering the slapstick tragedy of human reproduction. Victoria would have liked to ask Morris what he knew, but couldn't, out of love for him, over guilt. Her whole life she'd wanted to love Porter, and she did, but she could never take his side, because he kept changing his own side. His wasn't the only temper in the family but his wildness was his own. With Tammy dead, what would she and Porter have to talk about?

"You should take a break," said Victoria.

"Oh, no thank you!" said Morris in a pleasant tone of voice.

"It's hard," said Victoria.

"It's not," said Morris.

Victoria went down the stairs of their house, white-washed, which Tammy would not walk down again, nor touch the mahogany bannister. She went out the front door into the cold. She would call her husband and talk to Millie, now nine, whose voice always sounded so high and strange on the phone, then Porter, and they would worry over Morris and talk about Tammy, and they wouldn't be nice: they'd bring up their parents' various grudges against her, examine her unhappiness, which she had always been so generous with—she was still alive, they could be unkind—and what a fool henpecked Morris was, and what a fool she was to believe that at any moment Morris would have his long-awaited lucky break and become a successful actor, and in the end Porter and Victoria would have the same thought, though they couldn't say it aloud, not even to each other, and they didn't know that it was Morris's thought, too, and Tammy's last thought, flowing down her spine and out her fingertips with her soul. For once they all understood each other, the absolute astonishment: *To love another person like that! To have been loved!*

ELIZABETH McCRACKEN is the author of nine books: *Here's Your Hat What's Your Hurry*, *The Giant's House*, *Niagara Falls All Over Again*, *An Exact Replica of a Figment of My Imagination*, *Thunderstruck & Other Stories*, *Bowlaway*, *The Souvenir Museum*, *The Hero of This Book*, and *A Long Game: Notes on Writing Fiction*. She was awarded the 2026 PEN/Bernard and Ann Malamud Award for Excellence in the Art of the Short Story. She lives in Bath, Somerset, with her family.

FIRST EDITION
1 3 5 7 9 10 8 6 4 2

Library and Archives Canada Cataloguing in Publication
Title: Seven stories about Tammy / Elizabeth McCracken.
Names: McCracken, Elizabeth, author.
Identifiers: Canadiana (print) 20260189677 | Canadiana (ebook) 20260190810 | ISBN 9781771967594 (softcover) | ISBN 9781771967600 (EPUB)
Subjects: LCGFT: Short stories.
Classification: LCC PS3563.C3418 S48 2026 | DDC 813/.54—dc23

Readied for the press by Daniel Wells
Copyedited by Ashley Van Elswyk
Cover and text designed by Natalie Olsen
Cover image: Sektor Creative Design/Shutterstock

PRINTED AND BOUND IN CANADA